## THE SEVEN ON SCREEN

Enjoy another thrilling adventure with the Secret Seven. They are Peter, Janet, Pam, Colin, George, Jack, Barbara and, of course, Scamper the spaniel.

When four of the Secret Seven are chosen as 'extras' to act in a major new film, they can hardly believe their luck – especially as a famous actress is to head the cast. But on their first and only day of acting, disaster strikes: a vital part of the film disappears and the star of the film threatens to leave unless it's found. The Secret Seven are eager to help out but where on earth do they begin looking?

# The Seven on Screen

A new adventure of the
characters created by
Enid Blyton, told by Evelyne
Lallemand, translated by
Anthea Bell

*Illustrated by Maureen Bradley*

KNIGHT BOOKS
Hodder and Stoughton

Copyright © Librairie Hachette 1977
First published in France as *Les Sept font du Cinéma*

English language translation copyright © Hodder &
Stoughton Ltd 1986
Illustrations copyright © Hodder & Stoughton Ltd 1986

*First published in Great Britain by Knight Books 1986*

**British Library C.I.P.**
Lallemand, Evelyne
   The seven on screen : a new adventure of the
characters created by Enid Blyton.
   I. Title    II. Bradley, Maureen       III. Les
sept font du cinéma. *English*
843'.914[J]      PZ7

   ISBN 0-340-37839-5

Printed and bound in Great Britain for
Hodder and Stoughton Paperbacks, a
division of Hodder and Stoughton Ltd.,
Mill Road, Dunton Green, Sevenoaks,
Kent (Editorial Office: 47 Bedford
Square, London WC1B 3DP) by
Hunt Barnard Ltd., Aylesbury.

# CONTENTS

*Chapter One*

## EXCITEMENT AHEAD

'Ready, Janet?' asked Peter.

'Wait a minute,' said Janet. 'I'm just getting the ribbon properly fitted into place. Isn't it kind of Daddy to lend us his typewriter? It's quite an old one, so he told me I mustn't treat it at all roughly.'

'It *is* an old one!' said Peter, smiling as he looked at the typewriter his father used for the farm accounts and letters. 'Dad ought to offer it to a museum one of these days!'

'There!' said Janet. 'I'm ready now, Peter. Go ahead.'

Peter began pacing up and down Janet's bedroom with his hands behind his back. He stared at the floor. He was thinking hard! Then, still pacing up and down, he started dictating to his sister.

'SPECIAL IMPORTANT MEETING. Put that in capital letters, Janet. Full stop, next line. *All members to meet in the garden shed at four o'clock on Wednesday*, full stop. *Please don't forget your badges*, full stop. *New password* . . .'

'Wait a minute!' Janet begged. 'I can't keep up if

you go as fast as that! *Please don't* – don't what?'

'*Please don't forget your badges,*' Peter repeated, a little impatiently. '*New password,* comma, open brackets, SHOOTING IN PROGRESS. Put that in capital letters too, Janet.'

'SHOOTING IN PROGRESS – goodness, it sounds rather dangerous!' said Janet, tapping away at the typewriter. 'Won't they wonder what it means? *I'd* be frightened, if you hadn't told me!'

'They'll soon find out!' said Peter. 'Now, go down two lines and type SECRET SEVEN SOCIETY in capital letters too.'

Janet concentrated very hard on her typing. She didn't want to make a mistake right at the end of the letter. There – she'd finished! She took the letter and its four carbon copies out of the typewriter and lifted the copies off their sheets of carbon paper.

'Oh, bother!' she said. 'The last copy's terribly faint, Peter. I can hardly make it out – look!'

'Well, that doesn't matter too much,' said Peter. 'I'll tell Jack to come to the meeting myself when I see him at school tomorrow.'

'Oh yes – that's a good idea,' agreed Janet. 'Specially because then Susie won't have any chance of finding out about the meeting. You know she's always looking through Jack's things to see if she can discover our new passwords!'

Peter nodded, and while Janet typed envelopes with the names and addresses of the other Secret Seven members he returned to the newspaper lying on the bed. He was reading a news story on the second page for about the tenth time – he had drawn a careful line round part of it in red pencil.

It was well after four o'clock on Wednesday when Pam reached Peter and Janet's garden gate. She had been running so fast that her cheeks were quite pink. Just outside the shed, she stopped to make sure her badge with the letters 'S.S.' on it was still pinned to her sweater, and then she knocked at the door.

'Shooting in progress!' she whispered.

The door opened. Peter let her in, glancing round the garden, and then shut the shed door behind her.

'Late again!' said Colin. 'Five minutes late at least!'

'I couldn't find my badge,' Pam explained, sitting down on an old orange box next to Barbara.

'Woof! Woof!' barked Scamper the golden spaniel. He didn't like it when the children argued. He was bounding about the garden shed, asking for a game.

'Well, now we're all here, perhaps we can begin the meeting at last!' said Jack. Peter had told him there was to be a meeting, but he had gone very mysterious when Jack asked what it was about, and now Jack was on tenterhooks!

Looking very important, Peter unfolded the newspaper. Everybody else was watching him.

'Here, look at this!' he said. 'It's on the second page of the paper – the day before yesterday's paper, that is. I've put a red circle round the interesting bit. You can read it aloud to the others if you like, George.'

George picked up the piece of newspaper and began reading aloud.

'We shall soon have a chance to see our part of the country on the big screen. The famous film director Clifford Leigh is coming here to film those scenes of his next production that have to be photographed on location. The film is called *The Lady and the Highwaymen*, set in the eighteenth century, and it is about a beautiful countess making her escape from a gang of ruffians who are pursuing her across England. The first scenes will be shot at Covelty Castle – '

'So *that's* the kind of shooting you meant, Peter!' said Jack, interrupting. He looked a little bit disappointed – but the girls were thrilled!

'Do be quiet, Jack!' said Barbara. 'Go on, George, do go on!'

'The first scenes will be shot at Covelty Castle in a fortnight's time,' George went on reading. 'Many well-known actors will be in the cast, among them the famous film star Katy Kent, who won an Oscar last year in Hollywood.'

'Katy Kent!' exclaimed Barbara. 'My word – think of that! Katy Kent is actually coming *here*!'

'How exciting!' said Pam. 'She's my very favourite star!'

'Mine too,' agreed Barbara.

'What on earth are you two going on about?' asked Colin, bewildered. Obviously the name of Katy Kent didn't mean anything to *him*.

'She was the star of a film called *The Colonel's Lady*,' explained Pam. 'I saw it when they showed it on television one Sunday evening.'

'Yes, and I saw her in a film called *Island of Mystery* when I went to the cinema a few weeks ago,' said Barbara. 'She nearly got eaten by a lion!'

'Oh, I saw that film too,' Jack remembered. 'Yes, it was a really exciting one. She was taken prisoner by a tribe of Indians, wasn't she?'

'That's right,' Barbara agreed. 'She was simply marvellous – and she's awfully pretty.'

None of this meant anything at all to Colin! George showed him a photograph of the actress, a little further down the page of the local newspaper.

'Oh, is that her?' said Colin. 'Yes, she's not bad-looking.'

This was high praise, from Colin! Judging by the photograph, the film star really *was* very beautiful. She was blonde and bright-eyed, with a lovely smile.

'Come on, George, get on to the end of the news story!' said Peter impatiently. 'That's the interesting bit as far as the Secret Seven are concerned!'

The others were all passing the newspaper round to have a look at the photograph of Katy Kent. George got it back from them and went on reading.

'. . . who won an Oscar last year in Hollywood. The film also needs a large cast of extras. Mr Lewis, the film's assistant director, hopes to find them locally, and we feel sure that our readers will respond to his appeal. During filming, he is staying with his old friend Mr Fitzwilliam, the well-known landowner, and anyone who would like to act as an extra in the film should go to Fitzwilliam Hall on Monday, between four and seven p.m. Children are needed as well as adults, and a fee will be paid. So good luck to all you budding actors and actresses!'

'I say! How *exciting*!' cried the girls. They were really thrilled by the idea of acting as 'extras' in crowd scenes.

'A fee will be paid!' said George. He was treasurer of the Secret Seven Society. 'Our cash is pretty low at the moment – here's a chance to earn a bit more!'

'Film work is supposed to be quite well paid,' agreed Peter, 'but that's not the most important part of it. It would be a very interesting thing to do – and that sort of chance doesn't come our way every day.'

'Do you think they'd take all seven of us on?' asked Colin.

'Well, even if they don't, those who *do* get picked will contribute their fees to the Secret Seven's funds,' said George firmly.

Just then Scamper decided it was about time *he* said something. He barked very loudly, just to let the children know he was still there.

'Don't worry, Scamper,' Peter said, patting the dog. 'We won't forget to buy *you* a nice titbit out of the funds in the cash-box too!'


After school next Monday the Seven all cycled up to the Hall. They were rather surprised to see that there was already quite a long queue in the drive outside the door. Obviously they weren't by any means the only people who had thought it would be fun to be extras in a film.

They joined the queue themselves, and they had been standing there for nearly quarter of an hour when Jack's annoying little sister Susie and her giggly friend Binkie came along the road. They were going for a walk. When they saw all the people, they stopped to look – and saw the Seven in the queue!

'Ha, ha, ha!' laughed Susie, clinging to the railings that ran between the road and the drive of the Hall, and talking at the top of her voice so that the Seven could hear every word she said. 'Just look at them,

Binkie! The famous Secret Seven think they're going to be film stars! Fancy that!'

'Ooh, I say!' giggled Binkie. 'Haven't they ever heard you've got to be good-looking to act in films?'

'You'd have thought Jack and Colin might have scrubbed their finger-nails,' Susie agreed.

'Here, that's enough of that!' shouted Colin.

'Leave them to me!' said Jack grimly. 'You keep my place in the queue for me, Colin!'

But when they saw him marching purposefully towards the gate in the railings the two little girls took fright and ran away down the road, squealing.

'Just you wait!' Jack called threateningly after them. 'You won't get away so easily another time!'

But this time the two little nuisances *had* got away – and they were too far off to hear Jack any more by now.

The queue had begun to move rather faster, and when Jack rejoined the others they were nearly at the door of the Hall. Soon their turn came. They knew their way about the Hall quite well, because Mr Fitzwilliam was a friend of Peter and Janet's father, and Peter led the Seven inside. They were met by a young man who introduced himself to them.

'Hallo there!' he said. 'My name's Ben, and I'm Mr Lewis's assistant.'

He asked the Seven for their names and addresses, which they gave him one by one, and he wrote it all down. Then they had to wait at the door of what was usually Mr Fitzwilliam's study, where he and his estate manager dealt with all the business affairs of his land. But now it had been taken over by the assistant film director – the children could hardly wait to meet Mr Lewis and see if he would give them parts in Clifford Leigh's new film!

*Chapter Two*

## TAKEN ON AS EXTRAS

And they didn't have long to wait, either. Only a few moments later, a bald-headed little man came out of the study and invited them in. The children all thought he had a nice, friendly smile.

'Come along in, young people,' he told them. 'I'm sorry, it looks as if some of you will have to stand up – there are only three chairs in here.'

Peter remembered his manners and let the three girls have the chairs.

'So you think you'd like to act in our film?' asked Mr Lewis, still smiling kindly at the children.

'Oh yes, *please*!' cried Barbara.

'It would be fine if we could *all* be in it, sir,' said Peter hopefully.

'I'm very much afraid that won't be possible,' said Mr Lewis, sounding really sorry. 'You see, I've already got very nearly as many child extras as I want. I won't be able to use more than four of you – but I can see you're all great friends, so the other three are welcome to come and watch the shooting if they like. Just as long as you're sure to be quiet as mice!'

'That's a promise!' said Peter at once. 'Er – which of us *can* be in the film?'

'Well now, let's see,' said the assistant director. He didn't like having to disappoint *any* of the children. 'I expect you know it's a historical film we're making, set in the eighteenth century?'

Yes, the Seven *did* know! They just wished this nice, bald, smiling little man wouldn't keep them in suspense. It would be fun to watch the film being made, but even more fun to be really in it. Which of them would be chosen?'

'So you'll understand,' Mr Lewis went on, 'that I need to choose people who will look right in costumes of that period . . .'

'Oh yes, we do understand, but please, *which* of us are you going to take?' asked Colin, who could bear the suspense no longer.

Mr Lewis had wanted to spare the children's feelings, but he could see it wasn't any use beating about the bush. 'You, you, you and you,' he said, pointing to Colin, Jack, Janet and Barbara. 'But only because your hair is longer than your friends'.'

Peter suddenly wished he hadn't had his own hair cut the week before. George's hair was very thick and a bit curly, and never *would* grow downwards very much, in the usual way. And only the other day, Pam had persuaded her mother to let her have *her* hair cut short like a boy's for a change, and now she was regretting it! However, no one had time to give way to disappointment, because Mr Lewis was saying briskly, 'Come along, then, and try on some costumes.'

All the children followed Mr Lewis into the big room next door – it was really the dining-room of the Hall, but Mr Fitzwilliam didn't often use it as a dining-room, and now it was coming in very useful for the film people. It had been made into an enormous sort of theatrical dressing-room. There were dozens and dozens of costumes hanging from metal bars along all four walls. Some more costumes were still folded up and lying in huge wicker baskets, and yet more were piled on tables in the middle of the room.

A woman in jeans, who was obviously in charge of all these fascinating clothes, was shaking out the creases and putting the costumes on coat-hangers before adding them to the ones already hanging on the bars.

Mr Lewis introduced her to the children. 'This is Shirley, our wardrobe mistress,' he said. 'She'll find costumes to fit you.' He started to walk away, but then turned back. 'Oh yes, and I'll need the four of you children who are going to be in the film to bring me written permission from your parents, please, along with their names and addresses. The scenes you are to act in will be shot on Wednesday afternoon of next week, and you must be here at the Hall at one o'clock on the dot to get dressed and made up.'

'Yes, of course! We'll make sure to be here!' Jack promised, feeling very excited by the prospect.

'Will Katy Kent be here too next Wednesday?' asked Janet.

'Of course,' said Mr Lewis. 'As she's the principal character she acts in nearly every scene in the film.'

'And – er – what about fees?' asked George. He didn't want to sound grasping, but after all, he *was* the Secret Seven's treasurer, and it was up to him to keep an eye on that sort of thing.

'I see you've got your friends' welfare at heart!' said the assistant director, smiling. 'They'll be paid here at the Hall, when they bring their costumes back after the shooting.'

Then he went away, looking very busy, and the Seven stayed in the dining-room with the wardrobe mistress.

Shirley, the wardrobe mistress, had a good look at the four who were going to be in the film, and then she took several costumes out of a basket and tossed them on to one of the tables.

'Girls first,' she said, giving Barbara and Janet long dresses made of brown woollen material. 'And you'll wear these blouses under the bodices, and here are a couple of pairs of stockings.'

Janet and Barbara went into a little changing cubicle rigged up in a corner of the room, and Pam went with them. Jack and Colin were going to wear red tights, but the wardrobe mistress didn't need them tried on at the moment – she said she could tell the right size just by looking at the two boys. However, she got them to put on big, floppy blue tunics over their own shirts, and found a couple of wide purple sashes to belt them round the middle. Then she gave them little round, black felt hats to wear. They looked just like boys from the eighteenth century now – and were rather cross with Peter and George when they burst out laughing at them!

But nobody laughed when Janet and Barbara came out of the little changing cubicle again. They looked quite different from usual. The boys wouldn't have known them, got up in their pretty clothes. They were both wearing the same kind of long brown skirt, with a laced bodice, and a blouse under the

bodice. Barbara's blouse was made of pale green cotton with a lace collar, and her stockings were pale green too. Janet was wearing a lovely yellow linen blouse with little flowers embroidered on it, and she had striped red and yellow stockings.

'Over here, please, girls,' said Shirley. 'Oh dear – I think we need a few alterations to those skirts!'

She made the girls turn round and round in front of her until they felt quite giddy, and then she knelt down with her pin-cushion in one hand.

'Just a little shorter,' she said. 'It'll be much nicer then – we need your stockings to show to get the proper effect.'

She pinned up the hem of Janet's skirt, looked at it, and got to her feet again.

'There, it's just right now!' she said, sounding pleased. 'I'll take the other skirt up to match. Oh, and I was forgetting – we need something to brighten the costumes up a bit. Here, you pin this to your blouse, dear,' she said, handing Barbara a little spray of artificial flowers. Then she turned to Janet. 'Now, what about you? I know! Some ribbons – you can tie them into your hair!'

'What about shoes?' asked Pam. 'They're not going to keep their ordinary trainers on, are they?'

'No, that won't do,' said Shirley. 'A good thing you reminded me! Hm . . . let's see . . .' She thought for a few moments, and then turned to Jack and Colin, who were taking off their own costumes. 'Now, you boys – I expect you've got sandals, haven't you?'

'What, ordinary sandals with a strap and a buckle?' asked Colin.

'Yes, those will do nicely,' said the wardrobe mistress. 'Do you have some?' The boys nodded. 'Well, don't forget to wear them on the day of the shooting, will you?'

'We won't,' Jack promised.

'And as for the girls,' Shirley went on, 'I think there are some black ballet shoes in one of these baskets – they'll be just the thing. All right, you can all of you get dressed in your own clothes again now.'

What fun it had been, trying on the costumes! A few moments later the Seven were leaving the Hall. There were still about twenty people in the queue outside, waiting to see if Mr Lewis could give them parts as extras. There were four young men among them, with very long hair, playing guitars and singing American folk-songs. The Seven didn't know any of these young men, so they guessed that they must have come to the Hall specially to try to get parts in the film, and wondered if they would be lucky.

What an exciting day! The Seven talked and talked about it all, and it was getting quite dark by the time they said goodbye to each other and went home.

A few days later something unexpected brought all the boys at Peter and Jack's school running into the middle of the school playground at break.

'Look at those lights! Golly – what *bright* lights, and

in daytime too!' everyone cried. They all crowded together by the fence, craning their necks to look.

Peter and Jack had been at the other end of the playground, but when they heard everyone else shouting they came hurrying up to the spot where they could get the best view of the lights. Sure enough, the radiance was dazzling! It came from six floodlights on the hills outside the village.

'I know where *that* is!' said Peter, 'Covelty Castle, up in the hills there!'

'Then they must have started actually shooting the film!' cried Jack.

The two friends went off to discuss the news together, and Peter decided that a meeting of the Secret Seven Society ought to be held after school that day. If everyone agreed, they could ride up to the castle on their bicycles. Peter felt sure that nice Mr Lewis would let them come close enough to watch some of the filming. At dinner-time, the two boys hurried round the village leaving messages for the rest of the Seven – and so, at quarter past five that afternoon, the Secret Seven met outside Peter and Janet's garden, bringing their bicycles and all ready to set off!

A winding little road led up to the hills where Covelty Castle stood. The children had to pedal away hard, because the slope was quite steep. In the end they had to get off and push their bikes uphill. They were very excited at the prospect of seeing a real film being made, and were wondering about all sorts of things! Would they actually see the famous Katy Kent today?

'Yes, of course we will!' said Pam confidently. 'After all, Mr Lewis told us she was in almost every scene in the film, didn't he?'

'Then we'll be able to get quite close to her!' said Janet happily. 'We'll even be able to *talk* to her!'

'Oh yes, and what are you planning to say, exactly?' asked Colin, teasing the girls. 'I bet you anything you won't be able to say a word once you're face to face with your precious Katy Kent!'

'I can't think why you say that, Colin!' protested Barbara. 'She's another woman, after all – and we're not so silly as to be tongue-tied!'

'Look, there's Ben!' said Peter suddenly. He and Jack had been pushing their bikes ahead of the others, not listening to any of the teasing going on behind them. Sure enough, once they reached the top of the hill they all saw Mr Lewis's young assistant Ben, standing in the middle of the road and carrying a walkie-talkie radio. As soon as he saw the children coming he signalled to them not to make any noise, and once they reached him he told them, in a whisper, 'I'm very sorry, children, but you can't carry on along this road. We're shooting a scene in the castle courtyard, with the gates wide open. If you and your bikes got into the picture it wouldn't look very eighteenth-century!'

'No, it wouldn't!' agreed Jack, laughing. 'When *can* we go on, then?'

'They'll let me know over the walkie-talkie,' Ben said.

The girls took advantage of seeing Ben to find out if Katy Kent was up at the castle, acting, and if he hadn't warned them to be quiet they would have given shouts of joy on hearing that the film star really *was* there. Their happiness was complete when Ben, hearing that the 'take' was over, let them go on as far as the set where the film was being made.

The Seven left their bicycles in the ditch by the side of the road and started off towards Covelty Castle, almost running the rest of the way. What an exciting moment!

*Chapter Three*

# KATY KENT

When the Seven reached the fine old castle, they were surprised by the scene of apparent confusion that met their eyes! The courtyard was full of cables, lights, cameras, crates, trucks and trailers. A crowd of people were rushing about, talking about the filming in what seemed to be a special language of their own! At least, *some* of it was English all right – but then the children kept hearing words like 'zoom' and 'panning', and 'tracking shot', and 'filter' and 'dolly'. Janet looked round for a doll, but she couldn't see one anywhere! She asked Peter if *he* knew where the dolly was.

'Dolly?' said Peter, laughing. 'Oh, Janet, you silly thing! That's a kind of camera that gets moved in and out – I mean closer to or further away from whatever's being filmed. I read a bit about filming once I knew Clifford Leigh was coming on location here,' he explained modestly.

Even Peter, however, didn't quite dare to go on into the middle of the courtyard. So the Seven stayed where they were for the time being, watching.

'Oh, look at that man over by the foot of the tower!' said Janet. 'He's all dressed up in eighteenth-century costume – and listening to a transistor radio! What a strange sight!'

'And another actor's having his face made up just there,' said George.

'My word,' said Colin. 'That's the first time I've ever seen a *man* with black lines drawn round his eyes!'

'Ah, there's Mr Lewis,' said Peter. 'I'll go and ask if we can come in.'

He made his way through a positive barricade of lights and cameras and went over to the assistant director, who smiled at him.

'Hallo!' he said. 'It's Peter, isn't it? I'm glad you're

interested enough to come and watch. Are you on your own?'

'No, my friends came too,' said Peter. 'They're just outside the gateway. We're not sure where to go so as not to bother anyone.'

'There isn't much room, and that's a fact!' said Mr Lewis. 'But you can go over there – you won't be in the way if you stay near the generating unit. That big blue truck, I mean. The generator in it provides our electricity.'

Peter waved to the others, to let them know they could join him, and soon the Seven were sitting near the blue truck, staring at everything going on around them.

They saw three big, strong men – Mr Lewis said they were the scene-shifters – putting an enormous camera on a sort of little cart on rails, so that the camera could be moved backwards or forwards while it was taking pictures. As they listened to the assistant director's explanations, they began to understand a little more about it all.

'See that man sitting near the small table? That's the sound engineer with his recording apparatus.'

'What about the microphone?' asked Jack. 'Where's that?'

'Up there,' said Mr Lewis, pointing to a big metal pole several metres above the ground. 'It's on what we call a boom.'

Suddenly the lights came on. They were so bright and dazzling that the children had to close their eyes for a moment.

'Ready for the rehearsal?' shouted a man in dark glasses.

'Ready,' said somebody else near him.

'Who was that?' asked Peter.

'That's Clifford Leigh, the director himself.'

'What about the man who answered him?' asked George.

'That's the chief cameraman,' Mr Lewis told them. 'He's making sure the light's right for getting the best possible pictures.'

'Oh – there's Katy Kent!' Pam whispered to Janet.

'Where?' asked Barbara. 'Where?'

'Near the camera, talking to the director.'

'Are you sure that's her?' asked Barbara a little doubtfully.

'Absolutely sure!' said Pam. 'You just don't recognise her because of her wig and her costume, but it really *is* her!'

The three girls watched, spellbound, as the film star walked slowly towards the gateway, followed by the camera and a positive swarm of technicians. She started her walk three or four times, doing just the same thing each time – and then the director told someone to call Katy Kent!

Amazed, the three girls bit back exclamations of surprise. So the young woman they had just been watching as she walked about in front of the cameras for more than quarter of an hour *wasn't* Katy Kent after all! Who was she, then? They asked Mr Lewis.

'That's Maria, her stand-in,' he explained. 'She takes Katy's place while they're getting the lighting and the camera movements just right. There, look – here comes your star now!'

Sure enough, the real Katy Kent was coming out of her trailer on the far side of the courtyard. The girls recognised her at once! She was wearing a wonderful dress covered all over with jewels. She walked towards the director, looking very grand. And while he was

telling her the way he wanted her to act the next scene, Shirley the wardrobe mistress arranged the folds of her dress.

The actor who had been listening to his radio a little while before came to join the group and took part in the conversation. Finally, once they had all agreed on what they were going to do, the real rehearsal began.

Katy Kent walked slowly towards the gateway, just as her stand-in had been doing, talking in a low voice. The actor, in his powdered wig, was walking beside her, listening to her long speech with interest.

The star only needed to rehearse the scene once, so as to get familiar with the camera movements, and then she wanted it to be shot immediately. At the last moment her make-up man, who was called Johnny, came dashing up to dab a little more eye-shadow on her eyelids, and Shirley made sure her dress was hanging properly yet again. When everything was ready, the director called out, 'Roll!'

'Lights!' shouted the chief cameraman.

'Silence!' yelled Ben, who had come back to the set.

One of the scene-shifters held up a little blackboard with a clapper up to the camera. He said, out loud, *The Lady and the Highwaymen*, one hundred and two, Take One.'

Then he worked the clapperboard, which made a sudden loud clacking noise, and hurried off.

'Take!' repeated the director.

Katy Kent acted her scene, watched by the

admiring eyes of the Secret Seven. She really *was* a good actress! She had a beautiful speaking voice, full of expression, and she moved so gracefully you might have thought she was a queen.

Pam, Barbara and Janet were spellbound as they watched. But they came down to earth with a bump when the director suddenly broke the spell, shouting, 'Cut! Good, very good!'

All of a sudden two men came rushing up to the actress with their arms full of bouquets of flowers! They were talking a foreign language in loud, excited voices. '*Bella! Bellissima!*' they kept saying.

'I think that's Italian,' said Peter.

'Goodness!' said Barbara. 'I wonder what a couple of Italians are doing here?'

'Oh, I expect they're something to do with the film,' Peter guessed. 'The cinema industry is a very international business, you know.'

International it might be, but it wasn't quite as glamorous as the girls had expected. They had hoped to see more of the film than just that one scene, but now the director was making Katy Kent go over and over parts of it again, just repeating the same phrases.

'My lord,' she was saying to the actor in the wig, 'you must know that I have been entrusted by the King with a most important diplomatic mission! The information I am carrying to the Continent is of enormous value. And I know that a band of villainous men have been close on my heels since I left London. My life is in constant danger. Every road I travel is a perilous one; no inn is entirely safe. That, my lord, is why I am asking for your aid!'

The Seven could still hear her voice echoing in their ears as they cycled downhill again on their way home. It was a lot easier than the climb *up* to the castle! Night was beginning to fall, and they didn't talk much. They had such a lot to think about! And soon four of them would be in the very same film as the actors they had seen today – what fun that would be!

## Chapter Four

# THE GREAT DAY

At last the great day came! It was very nearly the half-term holiday, and so there wasn't much to be done at school in the way of real lessons, and the children had little difficulty in getting Wednesday afternoon off. Jack, Janet, Barbara and Colin went up to the Hall at one o'clock. There were a great many 'extras' putting on their costumes in the dressing-room, grown-ups as well as children. Of course, most of them knew each other quite well, because they all lived near the Hall, and so there was a good deal of laughter as they got dressed. It was funny for people to see their next-door neighbours, or people who worked in the same place, all dressed up in red stockings and plumed hats!

Colin noticed the four young men who had been singing to the accompaniment of their own guitars – so they *had* been taken on! Shirley, the wardrobe mistress, was tying back their long hair so that they looked like gentlemen of the eighteenth century. Janet tied a yellow ribbon round her own head, and Barbara pinned her pretty little bunch of artificial flowers to her bodice. At last everyone was ready They all went down into the village with Mr Lewis and Shirley, to the road where the scenes from the film were to be shot.

Jack and Colin used to go along that road every day on their way to school – but it was so changed they'd hardly have known it again! The surface of the road and the pavement had been covered up with a thick layer of sand, and pretty copper lanterns had replaced the modern street lights. That wasn't all, either! The children kept spotting more things that had been done to make the village street look like part of an eighteenth-century town.

'Look, there are flowers at all the windows!' cried Barbara.

'Yes,' said Colin, 'and the signs over the shops have all been changed, too!'

'I say!' said Jack. 'Look, the post office has turned into an apothecary's shop with huge coloured jars in the window!'

'And the Railway Inn's got a new sign too!' Janet discovered. 'It's called the Coach and Horses instead. I wonder why?'

'Because there *weren't* any railways in the eighteenth century, of course,' Jack explained.

'Oh, what a shame!' said Barbara, sounding disappointed. 'All those geraniums in the window-boxes are made of plastic. I thought they were real!'

Now all the extras, including the four children, had to wait about for the main actors to arrive, so that filming could begin. The camera was there already, with a lot of technicians doing things very busily around it. They and their equipment had taken over the whole road. There were film people everywhere: on the doorsteps of houses, perched on window-sills, even in people's front gardens, and they all seemed to have a lot of things with them. Most of the villagers, even if they weren't being extras in the film, thought it was rather interesting, but not everyone felt the same. One old gentleman called Mr Collings got very cross when he saw some of the technicians in his little garden having a late lunch and putting down their empty drink cans on the garden wall. He came out of his house to shoo them off.

'Go away!' Mr Collings shouted angrily. 'Go along, get off my property! And take your rubbish with you!'

And he swept the empty cans off his garden wall and into the road.

'No manners anywhere these days!' he said angrily, before he slammed his front door. Next moment the children could see him inside his living-room window, keeping watch to make sure no one came trespassing on his little front garden again.

Not long afterwards, Jack spotted Peter, George and Pam. They were making their way through the crowd of onlookers who weren't actually in the film, but had come to watch it being shot, and were allowed to stand on the other side of the road.

Peter, Pam and George noticed the transformation

in the village street too. 'I say – not a television aerial in sight!' said Peter.

'No – I suppose the film people climbed up to take them down, and they'll put them back again afterwards,' said George.

'Oh, do look over there!' said Pam suddenly. 'You remember those two foreign men at Covelty Castle the other day, Peter? You said you thought they were talking Italian? Well, there they are again, just outside the sweetshop. And they're carrying enormous great bunches of beautiful roses!'

'No roses without thorns!' said a cheeky little voice. Susie, of course! They might have guessed *she* would turn up. And of course Binkie was with her too, giggling like mad, as if Susie had made a very funny joke.

'So they didn't want you three in the film?' said that annoying sister of Jack's.

Peter, Pam and George pretended they hadn't heard her. They didn't even turn round when Binkie added, 'And you the leader of the Secret Seven too, Peter! I say, what a shame!'

But Susie and Binkie weren't getting anywhere – Peter refused to rise to the bait. It was the best way to deal with the two little nuisances and, when they got no response, Susie and Binkie soon tired of trying to annoy him and went away.

A few minutes later the watching crowd began to murmur with excitement – what could be happening that was so interesting? The children were soon to find out.

'Oh, look – here comes Katy Kent!' cried Pam.

The children had seen the film star's big black car up at Covelty Castle, and here it came again, turning the corner of the road.

As for Janet and Barbara, standing with the other extras, *they* had a wonderful view of the actress through the window of her car as she passed quite close to them. A chauffeur was driving, and Katy Kent was already in one of her beautiful costumes, with her make-up man, Johnny, sitting beside her. As the car passed those two Italians, one of them threw a whole armful of red roses on the bonnet of the car.

'I shouldn't think the chauffeur's very pleased about *that*!' Jack whispered to Colin, chuckling.

The two boys were standing a little way away from the rest of the extras – and they were the only ones to hear one of the young guitar players muttering, 'Fancy going about in a Rolls Royce when there are people dying of hunger all over the world! How can she bring herself to do it?'

Almost at once, the lighting came on, flooding the road with dazzling brilliance, and rehearsals began.

Clifford Leigh, the director, told the extras what they were to do. Most of the time they just had to walk along the road in a casual sort of way, like ordinary passers-by. Some of them were to gather in a little group on the pavement discussing something in low voices – whatever they did, they mustn't talk loud enough to drown out the speeches of the star,

Katy Kent herself. Other people were to walk out of the shops as the camera came their way, so as to make the road seem full of the hustle and bustle of daily life in the eighteenth century.

The four Secret Seven members found they were in luck. They had a really interesting little part to play in the film – and one which would let them come quite close to the film star. Clifford Leigh told them what he had in mind.

'Now, I want you children to be playing hopscotch in the road,' he said. And the four children saw that someone had already drawn a hopscotch course on the ground, in the slightly damp sand. 'You're absorbed in your game, taking no notice of anything else going on in the street around you. But when Katy comes running down the road with one of the high-waymen after her, and she passes you and your game, I want you to stop her, seize her hands, and make her jump along the hopscotch squares with you, right?'

The four children nodded, and the director told them his idea was to heighten the suspense of the chase with this little scene.

'The audience will be afraid the beautiful countess is going to be caught by the man who's after her,' he explained.

Barbara, Janet, Jack and Colin were delighted to think they would have a scene of their very own. Everything went smoothly during the first rehearsals with Maria, the star's stand-in. The four children threw themselves into their game wholeheartedly.

Some of the film people were quite surprised to see how well they could act!

Soon Clifford Leigh thought they had got the scene just right, and he called for the star herself. The children were rather surprised to notice how discontented Maria, the stand-in, looked as she walked away, muttering crossly, 'Here we go again – Katy's star turn, same as usual!'

Jack and Colin were puzzled. After all, being a stand-in was Maria's job. She did it well, too, and they would have expected her to enjoy it. Janet and Barbara were very indignant on Katy Kent's behalf, and looked at Maria as angrily as if she'd been attacking *them* personally.

Katy Kent soon arrived, and in her usual way she only had to go through one rehearsal. The four children were a little timid when it came to seizing her and stopping her as she ran past, and the actress told them they mustn't worry. 'Just remember you're enjoying a game!' she said.

Then the scene was shot – and after the first 'take' she told them they had been very good. They were delighted.

Then the second 'take' began – but it was interrupted by the sound recordist shouting, 'Cut! I can hear someone talking in the crowd.'

He meant the crowd of onlookers who weren't in the film, and were supposed to keep perfectly quiet as they watched. Mr Lewis was over on that side of the road, to make sure they didn't come too close to the

set of the film, and he knew who had been making the noise.

'Keep quiet, please, little girls, or you'll have to go away,' he said quite sternly.

He was talking to Susie and Binkie. The two little nuisances had been criticising Katy Kent's performance while the scenes were being shot. Peter, Pam and George, standing not far away, winked at each other. They had managed to get quite close to the camera. There was a fat man standing near them, smoking cigar after cigar. Mr Lewis whispered to the children that he was the producer of the film.

Shooting soon began again. Katy Kent went through the scene three more times, and when the director was satisfied he said, 'That's fine! We've got it in the can!'

Then he started planning out the next scene, while Katy went to rest in her trailer. Janet, Barbara, Jack and Colin wouldn't be needed any more, and they went back to the Hall to change into their own clothes again.

Half an hour later they got back to the village – and found that something very dramatic had happened in the meantime. The shooting had stopped. All the lighting was switched off, and the technicians had left their posts and were talking to each other in low voices. The director, the chief cameraman and his assistant were standing around the camera, discussing something in a very worried way.

Wondering what on earth had happened, the four children looked for Peter and the other two. 'Hallo – what's going on?' Colin asked, once the Seven were all together again.

'Somebody's stolen the magazine of film!' Peter told him. 'That's the container with all the film in it – and this one had the film with the scenes they shot this morning as well as the ones you were in just now. A whole day's work, in fact!'

The quarrel over by the camera was turning into more of a heated argument. Everyone could hear the angry things the three men were saying.

'It's impossible!' the chief cameraman was shouting. 'A magazine of film doesn't disappear off the face of the earth just like that!'

'I've told you twenty times already!' his assistant shouted back. 'I was going to put the magazine away, and I only left it on that little wall for a moment –'

'He means the wall of old Mr Collings's garden,' said Jack, looking the way that the man was pointing.

'Ssh!' hissed Peter. 'Listen!'

'I knew you were in a hurry for more film, so I got you that first, instead of taking the magazine straight back to our truck. And then, when I came back to collect it, it simply wasn't there any more!'

'Of all the stupid, thoughtless things to do!' snapped the director. 'Do you realise just what this means? I can't say I see much of a career in films ahead of you after a mistake like that, young man!'

'It's a disaster,' the chief cameraman agreed. 'We'll never get the scene shot again as well as we did this morning! The lighting was perfect; the set was just right; Katy's performance was one of the best I've ever seen her give!'

At that moment the actress herself came out of her trailer. She had taken her wig off, and her hair was tumbling down her back. Her face looked strained and tense, as if she'd just been crying.

The argument suddenly stopped. There was silence as the star walked up to the camera. Everyone in the crowd was watching with curiosity to see what would happen next.

'If you're talking about the farewell scene,' she said, 'the one we shot this morning, let me tell you that I am *not* going to shoot it again! Never!' And she raised her arms in a dramatic gesture. 'It's the best thing I've ever done! It was a triumph – the triumph of my art! And if that film's not found, I warn you, I'm walking out on this production!'

She marched furiously away, and shut herself up in her trailer.

This ultimatum caused great excitement. The argument by the camera broke out again more violently than ever. All the onlookers were full of interest and curiosity – until Mr Lewis firmly sent them home, saying there wouldn't be anything more for them to see today. Soon afterwards, the technicians packed up all their equipment and went off.

The Secret Seven were on their way home when they saw Katy Kent getting into her own grand car, the big black Rolls Royce, to be driven off to the hotel where she was staying.

'What an awful thing to happen!' said Janet to her brother as they walked down the garden path of Old Mill House, where they lived.

'Yes,' said Peter. 'But – don't you think this looks like just the sort of mystery for *us*, the Secret Seven?'

*Chapter Five*

# A MYSTERY FOR THE SEVEN

After school next day, the Secret Seven held a meeting in Peter and Janet's garden shed. 'Well,' said Peter, opening the meeting, 'it's twenty-four hours now since the film was stolen, and I've just been to see Mr Lewis to ask if it has been found yet. No trace of it, he said. So I think it's up to us, don't you?'

'Yes!' said Pam. 'We must do all we can to help Katy Kent! Just think how disappointed she must be. It's not fair to her at all.'

'Hear, hear!' Janet agreed. 'It will be a disaster if the film can't go on because the star's walked out – and I can guess *just* how she feels, losing her best scene like that!'

'I don't suppose we're the only ones who'll be trying to solve the mystery,' said George. 'The film people must have told the police.'

'Yes, they have,' said Peter. 'Mr Lewis told me he'd reported the theft to our friend, the Inspector. But that doesn't mean *we* can't have a go too!'

'It's not the first time we've done *our* bit to help the police – or even got there ahead of them!' Barbara agreed. 'Actually, we've got a good start this time – because we were on the spot when the theft was committed, or almost on the spot, and that's more than the Inspector can say.'

'This is all very well,' said Colin, 'but exactly *how* are we going to set about making enquiries? We don't really know very much about the theft, we haven't got any clues, and I'm sure the assistant cameraman can't have had anything to do with it. You all feel the same about that, don't you? So where do we start?'

'We start by thinking who'd benefit from the theft,' said Jack.

'That's not a bad idea,' Peter told him. 'What does anyone suggest?'

The Seven sat in the shed, thinking – and Janet hurried up to the house to get something to *help* them think, and came back with a big jug of lemonade and some iced cherry buns. Everyone agreed that this *was* a great help, and they sat there in silence, munching buns. Scamper wasn't used to all this silence. He started barking.

'Shut up, Scamper,' Janet told him, but she patted him lovingly. 'Or do you mean *you've* got an idea to tell us?'

'Woof, woof!' went Scamper.

'I don't think that's an awful lot of help, old chap!' said Peter, smiling. Then he went on, more seriously, 'Now let's see – a magazine of film can't be sold again, as if it were a piece of stolen jewellery. I mean, it's got no value in itself, has it?'

'Except to Clifford Leigh and the film people,' said Colin. 'It's *very* valuable to them – specially since it looks as if they'll never finish the film at all if they don't get that magazine back!'

'You mean someone stole all that used film with the idea of asking a ransom for it?' asked Jack.

'That's right,' said Colin. 'And if my theory's right, someone will soon be hearing from the thieves.'

'Well, it sounds all right *as* a theory,' said George, 'but it doesn't tell us much. Who could actually have stolen the film? Who'd *want* to?'

'Those four young men with guitars!' said Jack. 'Don't you remember what they were saying when Katy Kent arrived on the set, Colin? Wondering how anyone could drive about in a Rolls Royce when there were people dying of starvation, and so forth? You know, I can easily see how that could lead them to stealing the film!'

'Let's keep calm,' said Peter. 'I won't forget your idea, though, Jack. Those four young men didn't look at all rich themselves – their clothes were very shabby, and I'm sure they don't earn a lot of money for food. I can imagine their taking the film so as to hold it to ransom for a large sum.'

'I don't agree, Peter,' said Pam, rather surprisingly. Peter frowned slightly – he wasn't used to the girls contradicting him! '*I* think someone stole the film just to hurt Katy Kent. Remember how upset she was! I'm sure the theft was committed by somebody with a grudge against her.'

'I know what you're getting at!' said Barbara. 'You suspect her stand-in Maria, because of the way Maria was grumbling at the end of the rehearsal.'

'What did she say?' asked Peter, interested.

'She said, "Here comes Katy to do her star turn," or something like that – and she sounded very cross and discontented.'

'She's jealous,' said Janet. 'She's jealous because *she* isn't a big star herself.'

'Hm,' said Peter. 'Well, that's a second and perfectly possible theory. Anyone got any more ideas?'

'Those two Italians,' George suggested. 'They seem to be great admirers of Katy Kent – maybe it would even lead them to the lengths of stealing the film.'

'I don't really see the connection,' said Peter. 'What do you mean?'

'Well, then they'd be the only people in the world who could ever see the great farewell scene, with their beloved Katy Kent giving the performance of her life –'

'Oh, don't be silly!' said Jack. 'That's too far-fetched by half!'

'Well, there could be something in it,' Colin said. 'I don't think we ought to dismiss George's idea entirely – it could give us a clue. I read in a magazine about a pop singer whose fans actually snatched the shirt off his back at the end of a concert! Well, if *you* were a great fan of some performer, wouldn't you rather have a whole sequence of film with that performer in it than just a bit of a shirt?'

'You're right,' said Peter. 'That's our third theory, then. Let's sum up: we've got Theory Number One, the four guitarists, Theory Number Two, Maria, and Theory Number Three, the Italians. Well, it's obvious what you three girls have got to do – you'd better go and see Katy Kent.'

Pam, Janet and Barbara thought this was a wonderful idea!

'You can tell her the Secret Seven are going to help as much as we possibly can,' Peter went on. 'And try to ask her some tactful questions about her stand-in and her two Italian admirers. Got it?'

'Got it!' said Barbara, smiling broadly. '*I* think this is the best mystery we've ever had – or at least it's the most fun.'

'Now, as for you, George and Colin,' said Peter, 'you must try talking to the people who spend a lot of time with the star – like her make-up man, and the wardrobe mistress, and her stand-in too, of course. Meanwhile Jack and I will go and see Mr Lewis, the assistant director. He's very nice, and I'm sure he'll be as helpful as he can. Right, off you go, Secret Seven! We'll have another meeting later on today, after supper – here in the shed at half past eight. Password's still "Shooting in progress"!'

*Chapter Six*

## THE GIRLS ON THE TRAIL

The three teams set off on their separate trails at once. The girls wondered how they could get to see Katy Kent – would they be let into her hotel room if they just asked to visit her? It was a slightly alarming prospect, even though they were excited at the thought of talking to the film star.

'I know!' said Pam. 'Why don't we take her some flowers? I'm sure she likes flowers – remember how pleased she seemed with those beautiful roses the Italians gave her?'

'Yes, that's a good idea,' said Janet. 'I'll go and ask Mummy if I can pick some peonies out of our garden.'

She ran off, and her two friends waited for her outside the garden shed. Peter had locked the shed up, as usual, because it was the Secret Seven's own special meeting place. Janet was soon back with her mother, who was carrying a pair of secateurs.

'I think that's a very nice idea of yours,' she told the girls. 'I'm sure Miss Kent would like some flowers, and maybe they would cheer her up. Let's pick her a really big bunch.'

Janet's mother was very generous. She cut a dozen lovely peonies, a pearly pink colour, and then added some beautifully scented stocks to the bunch, and some pretty, deep blue irises.

'Oh, what a gorgeous bunch!' cried Barbara. 'You're a perfect *angel*!'

'Not really!' said Janet's mother, smiling. 'We can easily spare some flowers – our garden's full of them at this time of year. Now, come along to the house and we'll find some cellophane paper to wrap the bunch. I know I've got a big roll of cellophane in one of my kitchen cupboards.'

And soon the girls were walking through the village, on their way to the Manor House Hotel which lay just outside it. The Manor House was a very comfortable country hotel, and they had already found out that Katy Kent was staying there. They took turns carrying the lovely big bunch of flowers, and soon got to the hotel.

'We've come to see Miss Katy Kent, please,' Pam told the man at the hotel reception desk, in her very nicest voice.

'Miss Kent is not seeing anyone,' said the man, firmly.

'Oh, but it's *very* important,' said Janet timidly, from somewhere behind the bunch of flowers – it was her turn to carry it, and she was almost hidden by its size.

The man seemed amused, because he suddenly

smiled, and seemed a lot more helpful than they had expected at first.

'Well, I'll try for you,' he said, taking the receiver off the telephone on the desk. 'But mind, I can't promise anything.'

He dialled a number, and waited a few moments before speaking. 'Hallo, is that Miss Kent? Reception here. I've got three little girls down at the desk, who say they'd like to see you . . .'

There was a pause while Katy Kent answered. The man shook his head, to let Janet and her friends know what she was saying.

'Yes, I did tell them so, Miss Kent,' he said, 'but they were so keen to come up –'

'Oh, please, can *I* speak to her?' begged Barbara.

'There's one of them would like to speak to you herself,' said the man at the desk. 'Yes . . . yes, very well, here she is.'

And he gave Barbara the receiver. She felt very excited, and her voice trembled a little as she said, 'Hallo, is that you, Miss Kent? Miss Kent, we're the children who were playing hopscotch – you do remember us, don't you?'

'Why, of course I do!' said the film star. 'Why didn't you say who you were before?'

'We – we'd like to talk to you. Could we possibly come up and see you? It won't take long, honestly!'

'Of course you can come up,' said Katy Kent. 'Tell someone to show you the way to my room, and I'll see you in a minute.'

She had hung up the phone – and when Barbara put the receiver down at *her* end, she was beaming.

'It's all right!' she told the other two girls and the man at the desk. 'We can go up and see her!'

A page-boy in a red uniform took them up to the second floor of the hotel in a lift. Walking along the corridor, which had beautiful old oak panelling and thick green carpets, the girls thought the Manor House Hotel must be a nice place to stay. There were views of fields and woods through the windows, and it was all very comfortable and quiet. No wonder Katy Kent thought it would be restful after her busy days on the set of the film.

The girls felt very excited as they knocked on the actress's door and heard a voice telling them to come in. They opened the door, and then hesitated for a moment. Could the woman standing there in a pink silk dressing-gown really be Katy Kent? They would hardly have known her again without her stage make-up, and wearing dark glasses!

'Well, come along in, do!' she said. 'You can't stay out there in the corridor!'

Rather shyly, the three girls murmured, 'Good evening, Miss Kent,' and then Janet held out the big bunch of flowers.

'For me?' exclaimed the actress. 'Oh, how sweet of you all!'

'They – they're only out of our garden,' Janet ventured to explain.

'That makes them all the nicer. Real garden

flowers!' said the actress. 'How beautiful they smell!' she added, taking off the cellophane wrapping. 'Do you know, I love peonies – they're my very favourite flowers, and I almost never get given any!'

'You've got lots of lovely roses, though,' Pam said, looking at a dozen or so bunches of roses standing around the room.

'Presents from my admirers,' said Katy Kent. 'But you know, *your* flowers give me much more pleasure.' She went to put them in a glass vase, and stood it on the mantelpiece. 'There, look – see how much prettier peonies really are than roses, though you almost never get peonies in a florist's bouquet! They simply *make* you look at them!'

The girls were delighted that she seemed so pleased with their flowers. But now she turned to look at *them*.

'Now, I wonder why you wanted to see me?' she asked. 'Do tell me – but sit down first.'

Pam, Janet and Barbara sat down on a big blue velvet sofa opposite the actress. Barbara took a deep breath, and began.

'Well, it's like this,' she said. 'We, and the four boys, make up a secret society called the Secret Seven!'

She spoke so seriously that Katy Kent couldn't help smiling.

'I think I've met two of those boys, haven't I?' she said.

'Yes, you've met Colin and Jack,' said Barbara. 'They were in the hopscotch game yesterday too. And then there's our leader Peter, and George, who's our treasurer, and of course there's Scamper the golden spaniel too.'

'And what are your own names?' asked Katy Kent, taking her dark glasses off.

'Pam and Barbara and Janet,' said the three girls all together.

'Well, now tell me a bit more about the Secret Seven,' said Katy.

'We solve mysteries and have adventures,' Barbara explained. 'We look for people who've committed crimes and so on, and try to help people who need it, and – well, we just try to be useful, you see!'

'And we'd like to help *you*,' Pam went on. 'We've been thinking about the theft of that film, and we've got some ideas of our own about it –'

'Have you, indeed?' said the actress. 'May I ask what they are?'

'Then you *will* let us help you!' cried Janet happily.

'Certainly,' said Katy Kent. 'I think it would be rather nice to have children trying to solve the mystery for me – and I hope you get to the bottom of it before the police do! However, what about a little refreshment before we go on discussing it?'

The three girls thought they'd love a little refreshment – and Katy Kent went to her telephone and ordered three cups of hot chocolate. Five minutes later, a waitress came into the star's room and put down a silver tray with three steaming cups of chocolate and a plate of little iced cakes. It was quite a feast.

'Now, tell me about your ideas,' Katy Kent asked the girls.

'We *were* wondering,' said Pam, suddenly finding it a bit awkward to say so, 'whether you got on well with your stand-in?'

'Maria?' cried Katy. 'Oh, don't say you suspect Maria! No, I'm afraid that's no use. I can assure you that we're great friends – why, Maria and I have known each other for over ten years!'

Barbara didn't like to mention the cross remarks she had overheard from the stand-in on the set the day before.

'What – what about those two Italian men?' asked Janet. 'Who *are* they? We thought at first they must be something to do with the making of the film, but they don't seem to be part of it.'

'No – they're what you might call my faithful followers!' said Katy, smiling a little wryly. 'Their names are Remo and Angelo. They're brothers, and very rich – millionaires, both of them, and they put money into my films, so that's why they're allowed on the set the whole time. They've been after me, as you might say, for nearly two years, watching everything I film and showering roses on me! All those bunches over there are from Remo and Angelo! And whenever one of them sends me a bunch, there's a little card inside with a message in purple ink asking me to marry whichever of them sent it!'

'Goodness – and which of them *are* you going to marry?' asked Barbara, rather awestruck.

Katy burst out laughing. 'Oh, neither of them!' she said. 'Just think how disappointed they'd be if they knew me in private life – suppose they could see me like this, without any make-up on my face!'

The three girls thought this was all very exciting and romantic, so while they drank their chocolate Katy told them several fascinating stories about her life as an actress. She really was very nice, they decided, as nice as they could have hoped, and didn't seem at all inclined to put on airs. They thanked her very much for the chocolate and cakes, and for talking to them, and then said goodbye.

They went down in the lift, and were just going through the entrance hall of the hotel when Pam noticed the fat man who had been smoking cigars while the scenes from the film were being shot.

'Look, there's the producer!' she whispered to her friends.

The producer was talking to a man in a rather severe-looking suit, wearing glasses with oblong frames. They were sitting opposite each other at a table and studying some papers spread out over it. As the girls passed the two men, they caught a remark which made them prick up their ears.

'My dear Compton,' the producer was saying, 'when you make your financial report, do remember that you needn't hesitate when it comes to inflating the budget for the film. You know as well as I do that the insurance company's conditions are so tight, they positively force us to fiddle the accounts a bit . . .'

The girls couldn't stop and show that they were listening, so they heard no more. Once outside the hotel, however, they could discuss what little they *had* heard.

'What do *you* think?' Pam asked her friends.

'*I* think our list of suspects looks a little longer than it did!' said Janet.

'Just what I think myself!' Barbara agreed.

*Chapter Seven*

## AND THE BOYS ON THE TRAIL

George and Colin had found out that quite a lot of the people working on the film were staying at the King's Head Hotel in Belling, the next village to theirs. It wasn't so quiet as the Manor House, where Katy Kent had a room – and it was less expensive too, although it was comfortable enough, so the two boys thought they would probably find Shirley, Johnny and Maria there, and they wanted to talk to all three. They were in luck, as the hotel manager told them when they asked at the desk. He showed them the way upstairs, and they knocked at the wardrobe mistress's door.

'Is that you, Maria?' asked Shirley, inside her room.

'Er – no,' said Colin. 'I'm one of the children who were extras yesterday – maybe you remember fitting our costumes for us! My friend and I would like to talk to you.'

'Come in!' said Shirley.

The two boys opened the door, and found the wardrobe mistress and Johnny, the make-up man, playing Scrabble in Shirley's little room.

'Hallo, boys,' she said. 'You'll have to sit on the bed – there are only two chairs.

'Any ideas for a word of six letters containing a K and a Y?' asked Johnny.

'Kenyan, adjective,' said George almost at once.

'Terrific!' said Johnny. 'Hm, pity I haven't got all the letters!' he added, looking at his Scrabble tiles.

'We can go on with the game later, Johnny,' Shirley told him. 'Well, what is it, children?'

'It's like this,' Colin began. 'My friends and I are trying to find that magazine of film which disappeared yesterday – I mean, we're sort of investigating the mystery –'

'And we'd like to ask you a few questions,' said George.

'Anything you say!' Johnny told them, laughing. 'A couple of detectives in the making, eh? Carry on, we're listening!'

'First of all, could you tell us about those two Italians? You know – the ones who are always giving Katy Kent roses,' said Colin.

'What, you mean Remo and Angelo? Well, they're brothers – and millionaire brothers at that! They're head over heels in love with Katy. I should think they must have sent her several thousand roses in the two years since they've been taking such an interest in her.'

'Remember the terrace of the Ambassador Hotel, Johnny?' Shirley asked him.

'You bet I do! It was really amazing – you tell them, Shirley,' said the make-up man.

'We were in Brazil,' Shirley told the boys. 'Katy was starring in a film called *Sea, Sun and Samba*. She was staying on the top floor of the Ambassador, which is the best hotel in Rio. You could see right out over the bay from its terrace – it was a wonderful sight. Well, Katy will never let anyone come to see her in her hotel. So Remo and Angelo couldn't see anything of her at all on the days she wasn't filming, and do you know how they *did* manage to get a sight of her, and give her their roses in person?'

'No, but do tell us!' said George, quite impatient to hear the rest of Shirley's story.

'They hired a helicopter, and told the pilot to fly over the terrace of the Ambassador Hotel. Katy was in the swimming pool, right up on the thirty-fourth floor. When she heard the helicopter she thought for a moment it was an earthquake or something – but then she recognised Remo and Angelo as the helicopter flew low over the hotel, so she realised what was up! She couldn't help laughing, and blew her two Italian admirers kisses – and at that very moment they covered her with a rain of roses! You should have seen it! Roses everywhere, falling out of the helicopter and all over the terrace!'

'Goodness me!' said Colin. 'What a peculiar thing to do!'

'They'll do absolutely anything for Katy,' said Johnny. 'Do you know, they've got more than three thousand photographs of her! I've heard that they have an enormous, grand house in Florence, and some of its rooms have their walls completely covered with pictures of Katy!'

'I call that crazy!' said George, shaking his head. 'Do you think they might have stolen the film, though? So as to be the only people who'd ever see Katy's farewell scene from *The Lady and the Highwaymen*?'

'Well, as I was saying, they'll do anything at all where Katy's concerned,' said Johnny.

'Where are they staying, do you know?' asked George. 'I think we ought to go to their hotel.'

'Oh, they're not staying in a hotel. They've rented a very nice furnished house in Covelty,' said Shirley.

'Well, we'll go and see if we can find out any more there. We wanted to ask you about someone else, too. Someone you know quite well.' Colin hesitated. This could be a little awkward, if they were all friends! 'It's Maria – Katy's stand-in.'

'Goodness, I hope *she* isn't one of your suspects!' said Shirley.

George was feeling awkward too. 'You see, some of my friends heard her saying something rather nasty about Katy Kent, so we thought she might be jealous.'

'What a laugh!' Shirley interrupted him. 'Maria a thief? I'm afraid you're barking up quite the wrong tree there. Aren't they, Johnny?'

'Yes, definitely!' Johnny agreed. 'Maria's an actress – she's known Katy for years, ever since they went to drama school together. Katy's done very well, but Maria hasn't been quite so lucky. She's acted in a great many films, although never in starring parts. Recently she hasn't had many parts at all, so she agreed to be a stand-in for her friend – but as I said, she's a real actress all right.'

'And I'm sure you can understand that she's sometimes a little upset, because she can do much better work than just acting as a stand-in,' Shirley explained. 'It was very brave of her to take the job, if you ask me.'

At that moment somebody knocked at the door. It was Maria herself, back from doing some shopping. She said hallo to George and Colin, and then took two small parcels out of her shopping bag and gave them to Shirley and Johnny. They were presents for her friends.

'Nothing much,' she said, as if she was ashamed they weren't grander. 'But I found a shop in the village selling such pretty little models of animals! Now, what about a cup of coffee?'

The three film people asked George and Colin if they would like something to eat and drink as well, but the boys decided this part of the investigation wasn't leading anywhere much, and they wouldn't intrude on the party!

Peter and Jack had gone back to the Hall, because they knew Mr Lewis was staying there. They had to hang about near the gates of the drive for more than two hours before he turned up, though. It was after seven by the time the assistant director came driving up, saw the two boys, and asked them what they wanted.

'Oh, please, can we have a word with you, sir?' asked Peter.

'Right!' said Mr Lewis. 'Jump into the car, and you can come up to the house with me.'

He parked the car and took the two boys to the office that Mr Fitzwilliam was lending him.

'Now, what's it all about?' he asked.

'Well, the Secret Seven have decided to investigate the mystery of the missing film,' said Peter.

'You're not the only ones!' said Mr Lewis, smiling. 'We *have* informed the police!'

'Yes, we know,' said Jack. 'Actually, we've been quite a help to the Inspector several times before – we're all good friends! We only want to make sure that work on shooting the film can get going again as soon as possible.'

'So do I, I assure you!' said the assistant director. 'I'll be grateful for anything *anyone* can do! But this is evidently a rather complicated sort of case. There are no witnesses and no clues; there doesn't even seem to be a motive!'

'Money!' said Peter. 'We feel sure someone stole the film so as to ask a big ransom to let you have it back. Have there been any anonymous telephone calls?'

'No, nothing like that – or we'd know where we

were!' said Mr Lewis. 'Your friend the Inspector and I have been expecting some such thing all day, but no one's got in touch at all.'

'Is there anyone you suspect?' asked Jack.

Mr Lewis seemed to find this an awkward question to answer. 'Well, not exactly,' he said slowly. 'That's to say, it's far too soon to go naming names –'

'Those four young men with the guitars!' said Jack. After all, *he* was the first of the Seven to have picked them as likely suspects!

'That's pretty bright of you!' said the assistant director, rather surprised. 'Yes, you've put your finger on what *does* look like the most promising lead – because the fact is, no sooner had those young fellows pocketed their fees for acting as extras than they disappeared without trace! The Inspector's men have been searching the whole area, and there's no sign of them at all.'

'What does film cost?' asked Peter.

'Oh, not all that much to buy. What makes it valuable are those scenes we shot yesterday – which make it quite irreplaceable to Clifford Leigh, and Mr Bergson the producer, and indeed myself and all the rest of us. In this case, the film we've lost is worth even more, because Katy Kent has said she'll break her contract if we don't find it.'

Mr Lewis had only just finished explaining when Mr Fitzwilliam put his head round the door. 'Why, hallo, Peter!' he said. 'Hallo, Jack! Don't tell me the Secret Seven are at work on this mystery, are you?

The police certainly are – here's the Inspector come to see you, Lewis!'

And the Inspector came into the office, while Mr Fitzwilliam went away again, with a cheerful wave to the two boys.

There was a twinkle in the Inspector's eye too when he saw them. 'Got competition, have we?' he said. 'Well, well, well!'

'Have you got any news, Inspector?' Mr Lewis asked him anxiously.

'I do believe we're getting somewhere at last, sir,' the Inspector told him, beaming. 'You know those young fellows we were discussing – the ones with the long hair and guitars? Well, the baker's wife in the shop on the Renning road sold them ten large loaves late yesterday afternoon. She recognised the description of them one of my men gave her, and she says they set off towards Renning after they'd paid – so tomorrow we'll start searching the Renning area and beyond.'

What luck the Inspector had happened to come along just then, thought Peter and Jack! His information was well worth having! The Secret Seven would be exploring the Renning area themselves, next day . . .

*Chapter Eight*

## MORE INVESTIGATIONS

At exactly half past eight that evening the seven met in Peter and Janet's garden shed, as they had arranged. It was getting dark, and as there wasn't any electricity in the shed Peter lit an old oil lamp. The children thought it was rather fun to have such an old-fashioned and unusual form of lighting, specially as the flickering shadows it threw on the shed walls made them feel like conspirators meeting to discuss something of great importance.

Scamper was very interested too, and tried nuzzling the glass shade of the lamp several times, only to find that it was too hot for comfort. Very puzzling! He barked at the lamp enquiringly.

'Shut up, Scamper!' said Peter, taking the dog in his arms to calm him down. 'We've got to talk business, and not play games with you. All right, everyone, let's run through the suspects and see what we've found out. We'll take Maria first. What do you think of *her* as a suspect, girls?'

'Not guilty!' said Pam at once. 'Katy Kent told us they were very good friends, and had been for years.'

'She seemed almost hurt to think we could even *suspect* Maria of such a thing,' said Barbara.

'Yes, and Shirley and Johnny said a lot of nice things about Maria too,' Colin said, backing the girls up. 'They were really surprised to find her on our list of suspects.'

'We saw Maria, too,' George went on, 'and we thought she seemed very nice – relaxed and cheerful and not at all like someone who's just stolen a valuable magazine of film!'

'All right, one way and another that sounds as if we can definitely cross Maria off the list,' decided Peter. 'Now, how about the two Italians? What did you find out about *them*, Janet?'

'I think they're out of the running too,' said Janet. 'They're obviously a bit of a joke to Katy, but they admire her too much to want to harm her.'

'And they're certainly far too rich to need to steal the film and hold it to ransom,' said Pam.

'I don't know that I quite agree with the girls about the Italians,' said Colin. 'All right, Remo and Angelo are millionaires, so they can't have stolen the film to hold it to ransom. But from what we've all heard about them, it's easy enough to imagine them stealing it to add to their private collection of pictures of Katy Kent.'

'Apparently they've already got thousands of photographs of her,' said George. 'And the farewell scene from the film – the one Katy performed so well – would be the gem of their collection!'

'Well, we'll have to keep that possibility in mind and see where we get with it,' said Peter. 'Where are they staying?'

'They've rented a big house in Covelty,' said George.

By now Scamper had fallen asleep on Peter's lap. The boy patted him as he talked to the others.

'As for those four young men with guitars,' he said,

'Jack and I think they're the most likely suspects – Mr Lewis suspects them too. Probably they're silly, rather than really bad, and we ought to feel sorry for them. I expect they thought this was a good way to make some money – and I'm sure it won't be long before they get in touch and ask for a ransom.'

'Unless we can get on their trail first!' said Jack.

'Or the Inspector might catch up with them too,' said Peter. 'The police have found out that they set off in the direction of Renning, so we'll go and have a good old search around there tomorrow. They're very likely hiding out somewhere, camping, and that's why they bought ten loaves of bread. They wouldn't want to go too far away if they're hoping to get money for the film. Well – I think that's all we've got to say about the suspects, so now let's –'

'Hang on!' Pam interrupted him. 'It isn't *quite* all we've got to say – I mean, Janet and Barbara and I have found a brand new suspect for our list!'

This news created quite a sensation among the boys! Pam was rather pleased with herself.

'Who?' asked Peter, Jack, George and Colin in chorus.

But just then the Seven heard Peter and Janet's mother outside the shed.

'Are you in there, Secret Seven? Do you know it's after half past nine? Time you were in bed, Peter and Janet, and time the rest of you went home. Your parents will be wondering what's become of you. Don't forget, you've got school tomorrow!'

'Oh, Mother, just a little longer!' begged Peter. 'We're discussing something *very* important.'

'Well, all right – ten minutes, and not a moment longer!' said his mother. 'And mind you *are* out of that shed when the ten minutes are up, or I'll send your father to fetch you!'

'I promise we'll be out,' said Peter. He waited for his mother's footsteps to die away as she walked up the garden path and then said eagerly, 'Come on, quick – who's this new suspect?'

'It's the producer – Mr Bergson, isn't that his name?' said Barbara. She felt as proud as if she were a conjuror producing a rabbit out of a hat!

'But that's ridiculous!' cried Peter. 'I mean, the producer's the man who finances the film, or most of it. If *he* had stolen the magazine he'd have been stealing from himself, and what's the point of that?'

'But we overheard a conversation he was having with another man, who must have been his accountant, and what he was saying really *was* rather strange!' said Janet. She did hope the boys would take them seriously.

'What exactly was he saying?' asked Jack.

'Well, it wasn't terribly easy to understand,' Pam confessed. 'Something about the budget – inflating the budget, that's what he said – and the insurance company's conditions and –'

'And then he talked about fiddling the accounts,' said Janet. 'You can't tell me that *that* sounds like an honest thing to do!'

'No, it certainly doesn't,' Peter agreed. 'All the same, it does seem odd. If you're right, he'd have pretended to steal the film so as to get some money back from the insurance company. It still doesn't sound all that likely.'

'Perhaps he didn't actually steal the film himself, and he's just trying to turn it to good advantage?' suggested Jack.

'Well, I think we'd better tell Mr Lewis about it,' said Peter. 'Don't say a word to anyone else, will you? I'm sure we can trust Mr Lewis, but the fewer who know the better.'

'I say, I think those ten minutes are up,' said Janet rather anxiously. 'We'll *have* to close the meeting now, or Mummy will be really cross.'

'First we've got to decide just what to do tomorrow,' Peter told her. 'Let's see – Jack and I will go to Renning and search the place for those four young men. George and Colin, you go and see Mr Lewis and tell him what the girls overheard the producer saying. And girls, I want *you* to try getting in touch with those two Italian millionaires. Find where they're staying in Covelty and see if you can get them to answer some questions. All right – we'll meet at seven o'clock tomorrow outside the Hall!'

The Seven put out their oil lamp and left the shed. Outside, it was a clear, starry night. The children said goodnight to each other and hurried home, all of them feeling rather excited. What would tomorrow bring?

As soon as school was over next day, Peter and Jack got on their bicycles and set off for Renning. As they passed the police station, they noticed that the Inspector's car wasn't there.

'That means the police aren't back yet,' said Jack. 'And *that* means they haven't found the men they were after.'

'Come on, let's get going!' cried Peter. 'We've still got a good chance of finding them first!'

However, he and Jack stopped at the baker's shop on the Renning road. 'Good afternoon, Mrs Morgan,' said Peter, as he went into the shop. 'Could you tell us if it was you who sold some young men ten loaves yesterday? Young men with guitars and rather long hair?'

'That's right,' said Mrs Morgan, the baker's wife.

'We're looking for them, you see,' Jack explained. 'Do you happen to know which way they went when they left your shop?'

'Why yes, I do!' said friendly Mrs Morgan. 'It's a funny thing you ask that, because the police Inspector asked me the very same question. Like I told him, all *I* know is they set off towards Renning. But when my husband came back from his delivery round in the middle of the day, he told me he'd met them as they were going along the road, and they'd asked if there was a lake or a river anywhere near.'

'Paddock Pool!' cried Peter. Paddock Pool was a biggish stretch of water near the village of Renning, almost a little lake.

'That's right,' said Mrs Morgan, 'and that's just where my husband says he sent them. Well, I haven't had a chance to go to the police station, busy as I've been in the shop, and our telephone's out of order – if you happen to see the Inspector about you might tell him, would you?'

'We will!' said the two boys, leaving the shop.

They were smiling broadly as they got on their bikes again. Yes, they *would* tell the Inspector – but only after *they* had found the four young men! With the information the baker's wife had given them, they could go straight to their goal, whereas the Inspector must have been searching all day long.

The little country road they were riding along was nice and straight, and they could go quite fast. It wasn't long before they came to the spot where the road forked, and one of the forks led down to Paddock Pool. The two boys freewheeled all the way down the slope. They could soon see the water of the pool shining through the leaves of the trees beside the road.

But when they came out on the bank, they were in for a disappointment. A little way off, drawn up on the road where it ran along beside the pool, they saw the blue police car!

'Oh, bother!' said Peter. 'They got here first after all.'

'Look over there!' said Jack, pointing. 'The Inspector and some of his men, talking to those four young fellows.'

'Let's wait till they come back this way,' said Peter. So they got off their bicycles and went to sit on the bank. They played ducks and drakes with flat stones to pass the time.

Fifteen minutes or so later, the policemen started walking back to their car. Peter and Jack jumped up and hurried after them.

'Hallo!' said the Inspector. He was about to drive off, but he put his head out of the window to talk to the two boys. 'You very nearly got here first! But anyway, I can tell you it was a false trail. Those four lads are quite all right – they weren't running away from the village for any guilty reason; they just wanted to find a good camping site before nightfall!'

And he started the car up. Off it drove in a cloud of dust. There was nothing Peter and Jack could do but set off back to the village themselves, and it wasn't such a cheerful bicycle ride going home as it had been coming. They hardly exchanged a word all the way.

When they reached the Hall, the three girls were waiting for them and looking very excited. They came dashing up before Peter and Jack could even get off their bikes, shouting, 'Guess what! Remo and Angelo left these parts on the very evening of the theft! They aren't at their rented house any more!'

'Then we were right to suspect them!' said Jack, cheering up quite a lot when he heard this news. 'We've discovered that the four young men are not guilty – so it *must* have been the two Italians who stole the film.'

'Look, here come George and Colin,' said Peter, pointing to the door of the Hall. 'And Mr Lewis too!'

Sure enough, the two boys and the assistant director were walking along the drive towards the rest of the Seven.

'Hallo, children!' said Mr Lewis. 'I've been hearing about your suspicions — and I'm afraid your imaginations have been running away with you! There's nothing very strange about what you girls heard Mr Bergson say. It's perfectly normal for a film producer to want to make his expenses seem as large as possible — it's just the way he put it that misled you! If this film falls through it'll be a disaster for him — you can take my word for it; it's much more in his interests to find that stolen magazine than to get anything out of an insurance company!'

Yet another false trail! But that didn't particularly bother the four boys, who had never really thought very much of the girls' theory. All *their* hopes rested on the millionaire brothers. The question Peter was burning to ask Mr Lewis was on the tip of his tongue, and he asked it straightaway. 'What about the two Italians? Did you know they left immediately after the theft? How about *that*?'

'Oh dear — I'm sorry, but I must disappoint you again!' said Mr Lewis. 'They're innocent too, no doubt about it. I had a telephone call from them this afternoon, saying they had hired a private detective, at their own expense, to find the lost magazine of film. And they'll be back here as soon as we start shooting

76

again.'

'A private detective! Competition, just as the Inspector said!' said Peter, making a joke of it to hide his disappointment.

'Well, you've still got two days, children! The private detective won't arrive till Monday,' said Mr Lewis, and he went back into the Hall.

It was really very depressing! This was the very first time one of the Secret Seven's mysterious adventures had ever fizzled out in such a disappointing way. None of their theories had turned out right – they had all been proved wrong one after the other.

'I think we need to do some hard thinking,' said Peter. 'It's no use charging about we don't know where or how, trying to investigate the case. Tomorrow's Saturday. I've got to do some jobs on the farm for my father in the morning, and Janet has to help Mother in the house, and I expect the rest of you are busy too – but we can all think things over, and we'll meet in the shed tomorrow afternoon. I want everyone there at two p.m. on the dot!'

*Chapter Nine*

## THE ASSISTANT CAMERAMAN

The Secret Seven met at the garden shed next day, at two in the afternoon – and it turned out that while he helped his father in the morning Peter *had* been thinking, because he produced a brand new idea.

'You know what? We went chasing off in all directions in such a hurry when we started making enquiries into this mystery, we forgot to do the obvious thing!' he said. 'We should have asked the assistant cameraman some questions. After all, he's the person who's being held mainly responsible for the theft.'

'That's a good point,' agreed Jack. 'We need to get as close to the actual moment of the crime as we can.'

'Let's go and look for him *now*,' said Colin. 'We'd better not waste any more time.'

'Right,' said Peter. 'But we don't *all* need to go. Why don't you girls call on Katy Kent again? I should think she's getting a bit bored in her hotel, even if it *is* very comfortable, and it's only polite to keep her up to date with what we're doing for her. Or *trying* to do, anyway!'

'Good idea!' said Pam. 'Just what I was going to suggest myself!'

'We can take her some more of the pretty peonies from our garden, now we know they're her favourite flower,' said Janet happily. She was delighted at the thought of going to see the film star again.

So the Secret Seven split into two parts, and the girls set off for the Manor House Hotel, while the boys went to find the assistant cameraman, who had a small room in the same hotel as Shirley, Johnny and Maria.

The young man's name was Roger, and he seemed very pleased to have visitors. He'd felt too bad about the theft to go out of the hotel at all for the last couple of days! When he heard that the Seven were doing everything they possibly could to get the film back he cheered up a lot.

'But it's only fair to tell you we haven't got very far yet,' Peter warned him. 'Everything we've followed up has led to a dead end! So we hoped you might help us.'

'Of course I'll try!' said Roger.

'Right – can you tell us *exactly* what happened at the time of the theft?' asked Peter.

'Yes, it's not a long story. My boss gave me the magazine we'd just finished, and told me to bring him a new one as fast as I could. He was afraid it was going to rain. So I dashed off to our truck – we'd parked it in the road outside that crusty old gentleman's house! You remember, the one who kicked up such a fuss before we started shooting. I put the magazine we'd finished down on his garden wall, got some new film and ran back to my boss with it. And then, when I came back to collect the magazine I'd left on top of the wall and put it away, it was gone!'

'Who was near your truck at the time?' asked Jack.

'Almost no one,' said Roger. 'Wait a minute – I think I do remember seeing those two Italians somewhere not far off. You couldn't miss them really, not with their usual armfuls of roses!'

'I'm afraid they're in the clear,' said Colin. 'Think hard – didn't you see anyone else?'

'No, I'm sure I didn't. Only the old gentleman himself, watching us through his window.'

'Old Mr Collings!' exclaimed George. 'Oh, I'm sure *he* will be able to put us on the right track! He must have seen something – must have seen whatever there *was* to see, I mean. He was watching through his window the whole time, wasn't he? He never left it.'

'He won't tell us anything,' said Peter gloomily. 'I know the Inspector and Mr Lewis have tried asking him questions, and the moment he knew it was something to do with the filming he slammed his door in their faces!'

'It's our last chance, all the same,' said Colin. 'Come on!'

The four boys said goodbye to Roger and promised to give him more news very soon. Then they went off to see old Mr Collings. His house in the village street was quite a long way from the little hotel where Roger was staying, and as the boys went along they wondered what the best way of approaching him might be.

'Whatever happens, we must make sure he doesn't slam his door in *our* faces, the way he slammed it in the Inspector's,' said Colin. 'He's rather a peppery old gentleman, with strict ideas about good behaviour – so let's play *his* game!'

'What do you mean?' asked Jack.

'I mean we'd better behave the way he'd like young people to behave himself,' Colin explained. 'We must be terribly polite and tactful, and let him do all the talking. He was very cross when some of the technicians invaded his little front garden before the shooting began. But he'd have been perfectly all right if they'd only handled him with kid gloves! He's not used to people acting roughly – and people *do* tend to act more roughly and be – well, sort of more direct than when he was younger.'

'My word, you sound like a psychiatrist or something!' said Peter. 'But you're right, Colin. We ought to be extra-specially tactful with him!'

Soon the boys reached the little front garden of Mr Collings's house and rang his bell. Mr Collings opened the door just a little way and put his head out.

'Who's that?' he asked, in his quavery old voice.

'Er – could we possibly have a word with you, sir?' asked Peter.

'If it wouldn't be too much bother,' added Colin.

'Word? Word? What d'you want a word about?' asked the old gentleman.

'Well, that's just what we'd like to tell you,' said Peter, trying his hardest not to reveal the true reason for their visit before they were actually inside the house.

'Well, you seem nice-mannered young lads,' said the old gentleman, opening his door. 'You can come in, but mind you wipe your feet on the mat first!'

'Thank you very much, sir,' said Jack, stepping inside the house. Peter followed him into the front hall with Colin and George behind him. They saw about half a dozen pairs of felt slippers standing on its polished wooden floor. Jack hadn't noticed them, so Peter nudged him in the ribs! All four boys, unasked, put on a pair of slippers. They were big enough to go over their own shoes.

Mr Collings turned his key in the door again three times, and let the visitors into his dining-room. Jack, Peter, George and Colin shuffled into it in their slippers, trying not to look at each other for fear they'd burst out laughing. And this was not the moment for riotous laughter! They didn't want to spoil their chances.

The dining-room was very dark, lit only by a few rays of daylight that made their way through the closed shutters. Once their eyes had got used to the darkness, the boys could make out their surroundings better, and for a moment they felt they'd gone back into the last century in a time machine. The furniture was made of dark wood with brass fittings; there was a china lampstand, and old patterned wallpaper which might have been straight out of a Victorian house. They sat down on straight-backed, cane-seated chairs in total silence. It was a bit like being in church.

'Well, and what have you got to say that's so important?' asked Mr Collings.

'First, we want you to know we're very sorry about what happened on Wednesday,' Peter began. 'It must have been awful for you to –'

'Last Wednesday, eh? Don't you talk to me about that terrible filming business!' the old man interrupted crossly. 'What a harum-scarum set of people! Vagabonds, all of them! No manners at all! Good gracious, do you know I actually found someone had left his sandwiches in my petunia pots?'

'That was most unfortunate,' Colin started, trying to get a word in edgeways.

'Unfortunate?' said Mr Collings. '*Unfortunate*? It was nothing less than vandalism! And my pinks too, my bed of pinks – they trampled all over it without giving my flowers a thought. Unfortunate! Is *that* what you call it? Well, they can just go and vandalise somewhere else!'

'Please don't get so upset, Mr Collings,' said George, in his nicest voice. 'We've come to put it all straight. Your front garden could do with tidying up a bit, and once we've watered your pinks I bet they'll spring up again and be quite all right.'

'Yes, and we'll make sure we clear any cigarette ends away,' Colin added. 'You wait and see – once we've finished with your garden it'll look as good as ever.'

'Well, boys, that's extremely kind of you,' said the old man, mollified at last. 'I won't say no – it'd take me days to get the garden straight, for my legs aren't as good as they used to be.'

'Where do you keep your garden tools?' asked Peter. 'We'll get down to work at once if you like.'

'Come along, I'll show you!' said Mr Collings, rising from his chair.

He led the boys to a little yard behind the house,

where he kept his garden tools in a wooden lean-to. Peter handed out rakes and spades to his friends.

They made their way back up the corridor of the house, still wearing those comical felt slippers, and went into the little garden looking out on the road. It wasn't a very warm day, so Mr Collings stayed indoors, watching them through his window.

The old man was touched to see four boys putting in so much hard work, all for him. Peter watered the pinks carefully, and Jack tried to make them stand up straight by tying them to little stakes. George raked the gravel path, and Colin picked up all the rubbish lying about – cigarette ends, sweet papers and apple cores.

'Those people really *did* leave a mess,' he said. 'Really, it's too bad!'

'Yes, somebody ought to apologise. I'll have a word with Mr Lewis,' said Peter.

'Listen, have you forgotten why we're really here?' said Jack, a bit impatiently.

'No, but we'll get to that all in good time,' Peter told him. 'I bet you that if the Inspector had behaved more like this, Mr Collings wouldn't have sent him packing.'

After half an hour's hard work, the little garden looked neat and tidy once more. And old Mr Collings was smiling broadly on the other side of his window!

The boys put the tools away again, and then went to say goodbye to the old gentleman.

'We've finished,' said Peter. 'It's all in order now,'

'I don't know how to thank you boys,' said the old man, his voice trembling.

'Oh, there's nothing to thank us for,' said Colin. 'And I promise we'll get the film people to make you an apology.'

Peter thought the moment had come! He asked, in a casual sort of way, 'By the way, when they were filming on Wednesday afternoon, did you by any chance see a metal container lying about on your garden wall – a kind of biggish black container shaped like a figure of eight, with two little cogwheels on it?'

'Yes, indeed I did,' Mr Collings told the boys at once. 'In fact I came out of the house myself to pick it up and put it in the dustbin.'

'In the *dustbin*?' cried the four boys, horrified.

## Chapter Ten

## A LAST–MINUTE RESCUE

'That's right,' said Mr Collings. 'I threw it away in the dustbin, along with all those drink cans and plastic bottles. My garden looked like turning into a positive refuse tip! And the dustmen come on Thursday.'

'Yes, of course you *had* to tidy up a bit,' said Jack, hoping to cut the old man's story short. 'Well – we'll come back another day, if we may, to see how your pinks are getting on.'

'See you soon!' said Peter, making for the door.

'Goodbye, sir!' said George and Colin in chorus, as the boys went up the garden path.

Once they were through the gate, they took to their heels and ran as fast as they could, right through the village, out on to the country road, and to the Manor House Hotel.

Peter asked the man at the reception desk if he could talk to the three girls who had come to visit Katy Kent. He got his sister on the other end of the telephone almost at once.

'Hallo, Janet – is that you?' he asked, rather

breathlessly. 'Look, you'd better all three come down here immediately. We know where the film is. Quick!'

And he put the receiver down.

A moment later Pam, Janet and Barbara came down in the lift, and the Seven left the hotel at once.

'Old Mr Collings threw the magazine of film into his dustbin!' Jack explained. 'Our only hope of finding it is to go to the refuse tip!'

'We'll take Scamper with us,' Peter said. 'He might be quite useful. Better meet at my house in fifteen minutes' time, with our bicycles. And don't forget to put boots on!'

The Seven all ran off home in different directions.

Peter strapped a big basket to the carrier on Janet's bicycle – that was the best way to take Scamper with them. Scamper himself, watching these preparations, knew what they meant and wagged his tail happily. He loved going for bicycle rides!

'Come on, in you get!' said Peter, giving him a little tap. The spaniel didn't wait to be asked twice – he

88

jumped straight into the basket! He barked cheerfully as the other children arrived. The Secret Seven were all together and setting off for another adventure!

'Come along, Seven!' cried Peter. 'Off we go to the rescue!'

The sun had come out and was shining brightly, and the children cycled briskly along. Scamper had stuck his head out of the basket, and his silky coat was all blown about by the wind. The boys were in the lead, and the girls brought up the rear, singing in chorus.

The refuse tip was about a kilometre out of the village.

'Look!' cried Jack. 'I can see smoke – they're burning something at the tip.'

'We'll soon be there – and let's hope we can find the film!' said George.

It wasn't long before they reached the tip, an old quarry which was gradually being filled up with rubbish. The children set to work at once. It wasn't all that long since Mr Collings's dustbin had been emptied, and its contents brought to the tip by the dustmen's lorry. The Seven decided to search systematically, advancing in a line, quite close together, from one side of the tip to the opposite side. They would then turn and go back, and so cover the whole area.

It was lucky that Peter had had that idea about boots because they sank into the rubbish up to their ankles, and they had to leave Scamper behind. The tip didn't smell very nice either, and they tied handkerchiefs over their faces – that made them look like bandits, and they laughed a lot. It was amazing to see some of the things people threw away. They saw an old military cap, a coffee mill, a doll, some shoes that looked quite good, cracked china, an old pram, a car steering wheel, any number of bottles – but no sign of the film.

They had thought it would be easy to spot. This was rather discouraging.

'It'll soon be getting dark,' said George gloomily. 'And we've hardly covered half the ground yet.'

'Well, we can go on tomorrow,' said Peter. 'We mustn't give up hope. This is the only place where the dustmen empty their lorries, so the film *must* be here somewhere!'

Before they went home, however, the children visited Roger at his hotel to tell him that at least they knew where the film must be, even if they hadn't actually got hold of it yet. The young man was very pleased, and said he'd like to come and help search tomorrow – an offer which the Seven were very glad to accept.

Next day was Sunday, and the Secret Seven arrived at the tip at nine o'clock, as soon as it was open. Roger was there already in his little car, waiting for them.

Scamper had to stay on the edge of the tip again, and the children began searching where they had left off when it had begun to get dark the day before. Roger searched enthusiastically too. If he found the film, perhaps he wouldn't be dismissed after all – his whole career as a cameraman could be at stake!

Time passed by, and there was less and less of the area of the tip left to search. And *still* the children hadn't found the film! Their spirits were very low. Then, suddenly, Scamper began barking frantically and chasing up and down at the edge of the tip.

'I say, I think Scamper's trying to tell us something,' said Peter. 'Quick, let's go and see what it is.'

The Seven and Roger hurried towards the spaniel, and followed him as he raced along ahead of them. He led them to a remote corner of the old quarry which they hadn't yet explored. They saw two men in overalls searching through a huge pile of rusty old iron.

'Oh, please excuse us,' Peter said. 'My dog started barking as if he'd found something unusual.'

'Only us!' said one of the men, laughing.

'Do you often come to this tip?' Colin asked.

'Oh yes,' said the man. 'We're dustmen, see? Off duty today, so me and my mate have come out here totting. The Council gives us permission to do that.'

'What's totting?' asked Janet.

'Collecting things that might be useful, miss. Old iron like this can be melted down and used again, see?'

'Were you here last Thursday?' asked Jack. That was the day when most of the village dustbins were

emptied, and when they knew Mr Collings's rubbish had been collected.

'I think we did come along after work Thursday evening, didn't we, Bill?' said one of the men.

'That's right,' his friend agreed.

Heart beating fast, Peter asked them the all-important question.

'Did you by any chance see a big black container, shaped like a figure of eight, with –'

'With a couple of little cogwheels?' asked one of the men, interrupting.

'That's the one!' cried Peter. 'Then you *did* see it! Where is it?'

'Well, me and Bill, we didn't rightly know what it was, so we took it back to our hut.'

'Did you open it?' asked Roger, in suspense.

'I had a go, yes,' said the man. 'But there didn't seem any way *to* get it open.'

'Thank goodness!' cried Roger. 'The film's still all right!'

And he told the two dustmen just what that strange black container really was. The Seven joined in, telling their part of the tale, and all the trouble they'd gone to to find the film. The two men agreed to give them back the precious magazine of film at once. They had motor scooters with them, and they mounted their scooters and led the Seven, on their bicycles, and Roger in his car, to their hut on the edge of some allotments a little way from the tip.

How the children cheered when Bill and his friend presented them with the magazine of film! They thanked the two dustmen, and then went back to the village as fast as they could.

When they got to the Manor House Hotel the children stopped, but Roger drove on. He didn't feel like meeting Clifford Leigh, the director, yet, or his boss the chief cameraman, and both of them were staying at the Manor House, along with the stars of the film.

This time the Seven didn't even stop at the reception desk – they dashed straight to the lift, with

Scamper. The girls weren't nearly as scared of knocking on Katy Kent's door as they had been the first time they visited her!

The actress opened the door, and uttered exclamations of joy when she saw the magazine of film.

'Oh, well done, children!' she cried. 'I was sure you'd succeed! Come in, all seven of you, and I'll ring Mr Bergson and Clifford and tell them straightaway.'

'And don't forget to tell Mr Lewis – you could ring him at the Hall, where he's staying,' suggested Peter.

'And you must tell the chief cameraman too!' said Jack.

'And now you can all go on shooting the film again!' cried the three girls. 'Hip, hip, hooray!'

Quarter of an hour later there was quite a party going on in Katy Kent's room, all in honour of the Secret Seven! Mr Bergson, the producer, was there, and so were Clifford Leigh, Mr Lewis, and the chief cameraman. They all drank to the children, who had been so clever in finding the lost film. There was wine for the grown-ups, and delicious fizzy lemonade or ginger beer for the children, and Scamper wasn't forgotten either. Somebody had found him some dog biscuits, and he was happily crunching them up in a corner.

After everyone had heard the full story, Peter turned to the producer. 'Mr Bergson, I want to ask you something,' he said. 'Well, two things, actually. The first is not to dismiss Roger, the assistant cameraman, because it really wasn't his fault! And the second is to do something nice for old Mr Collings – I'm sure he'd never have thrown the film away if the technicians hadn't made such a mess of his nice little garden and put him in a bad temper!'

'Don't worry, young man!' said the producer, beaming jovially. 'Roger will keep his job on the film. As for Mr Collings, we'll make it up to him. And we'll make sure our people are more considerate in future when we're filming on location! How do you think the old gentleman would like a present of a nice garden seat?'

'Oh, that would be just the thing, sir!' cried Peter, delighted.

'Yes,' said Jack. 'Then he could sit comfortably in his front garden, and look at his flowers growing, and watch the world go by! *What* a good idea!'

'And how about you young people?' said Clifford Leigh, the director. 'What can we give *you*?'

'We don't want anything, sir!' Peter hastened to assure him. 'We're just glad we could be useful and save the film.'

'But we should really like to give you a present!' said Mr Bergson. 'I was thinking you might like a cine-camera.'

'A cine-camera?' breathed Peter.

'Yes, and then you could take your own films. And you'd better have a projector too, so that you can show the films at the meetings of your society.'

'Oh, that would be marvellous!' cried the Seven.

'Good – then that's settled!' said Mr Bergson.

Scamper barked happily too, seeing that his friends all seemed very pleased about something.

'Now,' said Katy Kent, 'I've rung down to the manager of the hotel, and asked for a specially good lunch to be served for all of us – so I think it's time to go and eat it!'

It *was* a specially good lunch too – roast chicken, and delicious young vegetables, and strawberries and ice cream for pudding. And the next week, just after the filming on location had been completed and all the film people had gone away again, several enormous parcels arrived for the Seven.

They held a meeting in the garden shed – Peter wasn't going to open the parcels until everyone was there! However, they had a very good idea what they must contain – and sure enough, out came a splendid cine-camera, with a good supply of film, and a projector.

'Come on!' said Pam. 'We can try our own hand at film-making – let's start straightaway!

'Yes, let's!' everyone agreed. They put a film in the camera, and Peter picked it up, took three steps backwards to make sure he had all his friends in the picture, and then called happily, 'Silence, everyone! Now – what was our password again?'

'Shooting in progress!' everyone shouted in chorus.